Rurality

Poetry From Beyond The City Lights

JR. Cleckler

Table of Contents

Beginning

And so now I begin, a new chapter, a new stanza,
A journey long contemplated but fearfully delayed,
Stalled by uncertainty, held back by responsibility.
The accessories of a normal life encumbering with chains
Well-meaning and not intrinsically undesirable,
Yet still restraining the racing flow of creativity.
The patterns established by culture and familial affinity
Have too long set a path not unpleasant but not fulfilling.
How to compose this new verse without losing the song
already written?
How should the colors new blend to accent those on the
canvas now?
The path before me beckons with possibility,
Harpies of failure scream overhead and behind,
But I must go forward into the unknown,
If not now, when?
One step to
Begin.

I Found a Poem I Wrote

I found a poem I wrote today,
Dreams fell tumbling from the closet of my mind,
Thoughts of what would become,
Thoughts of what could have been,
Falling at my feet like tiny scraps of paper,
Twisting and turning in the nocturnal breeze.

Untitled

Where am I?
For so long I felt like Sisyphus,
Pushing that boulder up a hill
Only to watch it roll back down again.
I thought the flame had died out,
Reduced only to a dying coal
Slowly slipping into a long darkness
Trying my best to provide some warmth
To those I love.
But something changed.
Suddenly the boulder made it to the top,
A flame burst from the dying coal
Now to give both light and warmth
To the loved in my life.
A fire burning hot, bright, and equal
For those around me.
I don't know what happened,
I don't know how it changed,
But I am not where I was,
And for that, I am happy

Shutdown

I don't know how to do this.
Water, the most wonderful substance on the planet,
Made of 2 H and 1 O.
There's a part of us missing,
Some special piece no longer close,
Unable to touch, unable to feel or hold close.
How long can a day be?
How many empty moments does a night hold?
Carbon 1, oxygen 2, three parts to the whole.
Whining…maybe.
Wanting it all…certainly.
Missing some special something
That makes a day seem a moment and the nights…
A star-filled blanket of comfort beyond imagining.
It is a season with no end in sight.

Night

Moonlight
Soft glowing silver
On the leaves
A breeze
Gentle caress on your lips
Touching your soul
And mine

Before Dawn

A whip-poor-will calls from not far away
Answered by the owl close by.
Sunlight not yet pinking the sky
While the moon slowly sinks in the west.
Thoughts run like the river
Deep and quiet over the rock I was
My heart warmer than the morning chill.
Alone, I stand beneath the glittered sky
Chasing dreams I haven't dared to dream

A Moment

A seemingly simple choice
A moment frozen in time
When everything changed
In a moment.
Outside this fragment
Nothing changed, no
Discernable, catastrophic
Consequences or calamity
When everything changed
In a moment.
Peaceful evenings of joy
And comfort dance over
A troubled heart fearful for
What might now be the new
Reality of whys and what-ifs
Memories of that seemingly simple choice
An instant frozen in time
When everything changed
In a moment.

Unseen

There exists the realm unseen
Those invisible bonds that bind
Holding us together with emotions
Drifting in the aether that surrounds
a place where thoughts have mass
Indiscernible feelings hiding,
Dancing from heart to heart without
Revealing to the logical,
The conscious understanding leaving
The speech centers of the brain
Unable to make the mind grasp
The wispy, light, emotional realm
That surrounds us
Unseen

Background Noise

Soundtrack to my existence
A dull, distant drumbeat
Made of electrical images and sounds
Bombarding
pounding
ripping
Insinuating itself into the sphere of my being
Drawing me like taffy
Stretching
pulling
tearing
Me away from the desire of my heart
Pouring a fog over what might have been

Is It?

Is it important?
Does it carry some intrinsic value?
What worth have I assigned to this thing I hold so dear?

Is it truly dear?
Close to the emotional, illogical heart?
Can something lacking physical presence affect the hard
reality we walk every day?

Is it critical?
Does the absence of the thing shape the world around it?
Do the missing pieces leave a void that cannot be filled by
mundane, monotonous beings?

Is it?

Yes.

It is.

Empty Silence

A whispered "okay" echoes.
Bouncing off the empty walls
Covering, surrounding the
Empty
Silent
Void
Within which would so soon
Ripple laughter and love, joyous peace
Filling the empty silence

Mountaintop

Clouds race by me atop the mountain
Joy beyond
Above
More
Than I have ever held
Cuddling me with strong arms of love
And togetherness gentler than softest
Down.
Rumbles beneath unsteady feet
Frighten
Trouble
Scare me, a portent of loss and a fall
Far beyond imagining,
more devastating
For the heights fading fast from view
As the mountaintop slips my grasp

A Distance So Minute

A distance so minute
Yet vast beyond all measure
Held close by darkness, soft and warm
But so far away
Quantum fields of love and loss
So tiny binding all together
Some distances so small
Yet still distance, after all

What Should I Be

14

Am I what I should be?
Must the path laid down before me be followed
Step by step without question or turning?
Am I what is expected?
Do I meet the requirements of those I hold most dear?
Must I measure up to the rule not made by me
without
thought or conviction?
Am I what I should be?

Rain

15

Rainy rhythm rolling over me
Washing cares and worry away
Arms wrapped around your waist
As I nuzzle close against your back
The smell of you drawing me in
To dance amidst golden
Flowers of dream.

Just the Sound

It's not the words
Talking about the everyday mundane
Silly, boring nothings that fill
The interminable hours making the
Days crawl by.
It's the sound of your voice.
The joy of a laugh ringing over
The washer or talking about the clothes
Folded before us in stacks to be put away later when quiet
time comes.
Waves in the air carry feeling across
The space between us but it's
Just the sound

First Date

I want to hold you as we watch the moon
I want to smell your hair as the stars dance overhead,
To feel your touch as the wind whispers
Above and remember your voice in the lonely day.
To dream again of what could be,
Dream once more

(The First Date)

Dreams of Three

Why does it seem so empty?
We do the same things as always
Enjoyment once found in song
Or wrapped in your arms at rest
Now not quite right, missing some
Indefinable element, some mysterious
Touch joining souls in the magic arcane

A seat with two legs, unbalanced
Steadied by the addition of one.
Two points connected, linear only,
Suddenly, a shape when another point
Drops from the heavens, making the
Two, somehow more than before.

Ice becomes water, becomes steam
Three separate forms but the same soul
Separate yet joint being, magical,
Complex and tantalizingly sweet
Whispered music playing on heartstrings
Threefold, making a chord eternal

When I Can't

I don't feel it right now.
The…whatever it was that let me write
Has been consumed by worry.
The crushing responsibility of
Everyday bill paying and grocery shopping and car driving
and on and on
Squeezing the inspiration from me like blood from a turnip.
I feel the creative juices flowing down
My soul from a deepening wound I could not anticipate,
no tourniquet to stop the losses and save what is left.
When I can't, I think of you.
When I can't, I make it happen for you.
When I can't, I feel you wrap the warm blanket of your
love around me
Cuddling me with beauties beyond imagining.
When I can't, you make me feel I can.

Thoughts

Flipping channels absently, not really
Seeing what is flashing across
A pointless screen stuck in the middle
Of the longest month in the history of time behind
an invisible barrier of little bugs keeping us all apart
for too long.
Scrolling through empty spaces, waiting
Until this all passes, when we can be
United once
more.
Thinking thoughts of us,
Thoughts of you, thoughts of what could be,
may
be, hoped for, dreamed of,
Thoughts consuming my nights

Quickly

How did it happen so fast?
I can't understand the mechanism.
Prying open a closed and frozen heart.
For so long, frost sealed my feelings
Behind cold walls until you brought
Light and fire, warmth and sunshine
Into my life, suddenly opening me
To a world of possibilities undreamed
Quickly carrying me into a new reality
More wondrous than anything I could have hoped to
inhabit.

Strangely

Strangely, just hearing your voice
Coming from that tiny little phone
Across the room makes it better.
Somehow, knowing that you want to call
And hear us is a comfort in troubled time
Laughter without me does not harm
Joy splashes like rocks in puddles
Sprinkling the surrounding grass
Crystal dewdrops of love glisten
In the spring sunshine

Remember

I remember the first time I saw you,
Scent of peach blossoms in the midday
Sun, perfume carrying over the roses, those two big
pecan trees behind you
Framing your beautiful face and form in dark green glory,
image haunting me for years.

I remember the first time I truly saw you,
Eyes hazel and star-flecked, drawing me across the
sales counter, the smell of paint mixing and pesticides
lingering in my nose, colors profound and plain spattered
on khakis
worn only for that purpose,
somehow losing myself in your smile and laugh, lifting me
above it all.

I can see us together in visions, dancing
Across snowy fields arm in arm, holding
Each other close against winter's chill, breathing in
your scent and feeling your touch on my soul.

What It's About

24

It's not about that for me,
Sure, that plays a part in it,
That always sits in the back of my mind
That is, of course, very pleasant and
Adds something to it, but that's not it.

It's more about the closeness for me,
The quiet moments of a simple touch,
The small movement, hand in hand,
Brushing hair out of your face,
Scratching that place you can't reach,
Catching the scent of your hair as I walk by on the
way to the kitchen,
Holding you close as night clothes the sky in a
starry shroud to be reborn with dawn's first kiss.

That's what it's about for me.

Muses

Inspiration comes to me from the aether,
pouring
over me like hot water from the shower runs
glistening over your body,
steam rolling up around
us
fogging the mirrors of our souls,
hot breath
mingles
With bodies entwined,
sticky with sweat,
waiting for
cleansing beneath waters
hot from desire, thought
pushing me further than I dreamed,
deeper than I
dared hope.

How Long?

How long can this last?
This feeling that consumes my thoughts
And fills my heart with joy I've never known.
Warmth and peace wrap me in a thick blanket
through the cold nights
Making the days rush by and stretch
Endlessly at the same time.
Rushing by in your
presence,
dragging on without you by my side.
But it can't last.
It won't be here forever.
Fear slips in on silent feet
warning of
The loss that must come,
the loss of those I hold closest.
Something will
Interfere,
some *thing* will cut these cords as a
dagger slices into my soul.
Will I screw it up?
Will my words betray me and
destroy it all?
This feeling has always slipped away
before,
this peace has never held sway but for a
little while.

I hold too tightly, and breath is crushed from my
lungs,
I loosen my grip, and love runs through my
fingers like sand.
I want this forever,
I can't lose this.
How long can it last?

Fear

I'm scared. I'm a grown man, but I'm afraid.
I cannot give in and reveal what haunts my dreams
at night,
distracts me while I wait for the sunset to
usher in the cloak of night to dream of you once
more.
I'm afraid to tell you how deep this river of emotion
runs,
how hot the fire burns when I think of us
together.
If you knew the way I feel,
Would you turn from me and run away?
Does the pain of your absence make me
Unstable,
unwilling to imagine a life without you to
hold in the darkness?
I must temper this passion,
quench this fire before
it burns all caution.
Careful,
slowly letting you see how much you mean
to me

Under the Influence

You have become necessary to me,
Something I must have every day.
Physical symptoms accompany the
Lack of your voice, a knot in my gut,
A tightness in my chest, an ache in my
Heart for missing you.
I am under your influence henceforth,
No treatment center can remove your touch from
my soul,
no antidote for your
Love.

Night

Warm south winds move the trees.
As I hold your hand, leaves twist with
The force of my feeling for you.
Slowly, we move to that place of sensual
Delight, our bodies pressed tight against
Each other, my hands exploring your curves, my lips
caress yours as wonders
Reveal themselves to my touch.
Hot breath against my neck as I hold
You close, your hair brushing my face
As clothing becomes a hindrance.
Skin on skin, flesh on flesh, stars an audience to our love.

Word Doodles

Civilization crumbling beneath the weight of ignorance and intolerance.

Diamonds peeking through the pinholes in the cloak of night.

Love glows like dawn's first kiss on the eastern horizon.

Emotions surging as waves crashing against a barren rocky shore.

Peace deeper than the mighty river flowing through fertile lands, green with new life.

Evening

32

Golden sunset radiance pours through wispy cirrus
clouds,
dripping glory into a dull monotony of
another empty day.
Cascades of emotion splash me into pools of joy
and love deeper and more marvelous than any ever known.
Dreams of your touch, us together
under midnight
black skies sparkling with diamonds from light
years away,
galaxies beyond time wait for our
eternity.

Thinking

It's dangerous sometimes,
Thinking like this.
Following dreams, believing they could come true.

Focus on the real, take care of your responsibility,
don't try to make what cannot come to pass.

Do I envy the limited choices of the simple life?
When there is only one path, the decisions are made
before a choice is seen. If only two roads diverged,
if only I could go right or left. But I stand in a
roundabout,
paths radiating before me like spokes
from a wheel,
turning,
spinning,
changing with each
passing day.
Simple choices, take care of you and yours.
Follow your dreams, come what may,
consequences
be damned.
Freeze immobile,
caught as an animal in the
On rushing light of futures uncertain.

For My Girls

They're fourteen and ten, and Daddy can do no wrong now.
The youngest said the other day, "Just ask Daddy. He
knows everything."
The older one still comes
up for hugs when I come in from work.
If I were a scientist, I would invent a pill that would
freeze time and keep them like this forever…
but time
stands still for no man.
I worry. I dread. I know soon I will turn into the old
idiot that doesn't know anything,
the one who just
doesn't understand.
I remember when my father didn't know anything,
and I remember when I knew just how much
wisdom he possessed.
Now I'm the father, and I know the reason for the
journey ahead, but, oh, the pain to come.
Will I know when I become stupid?
Will I realize that I don't understand anything?
How long will it take for me to regain my brain?
How long before I understand again?
One thing is for sure, the love I felt the first time I held
their tiny form will never fade.
The place where those tiny hands carved in my heart will
always remain.
A love beyond anything else,
unknown except to
parents,

that love holds true.
Forever.

Slow Dance

The lights slowly dim as the music begins,
Soft piano with gentle brushes on the snare drum
keeping time,
The baritone sax draws us close and onto the floor,
Swaying from cheek to cheek in the moonlight, falling
through windows high above,
Being enchanted by the scent in the air,
We move with tiny steps down love's path,
Guided by feelings too precious to voice,
Too fragile to express in mere words,
Best conveyed with soft caress and gentle touch,
As we dance to the music of the stars.

Options

Somehow, I feel free now,
Not chained to the everyday grind,
Get up, go to work, come home, go to bed, get up,
go to work, come home, go to bed. Lather, rinse,
repeat ad nauseum.
But now, we have family time, time to play with the
kids, time to cook meals together, time to just…
be.
But on the horizon looms the return to what was,
the grinding monotony sucking this new life from
our souls,
the pressure to meet expectations from
someone else,
driving ourselves to madness for
little green pieces of paper
we trade for food or
shelter
while losing the value of time with those we
love.
Are there options?
Could it be different?
Instead of punching a clock,
can I trade words for those
cursed paper valuables?
Is my music worth more than the manufactured
consumables my clock-punching produced?
Could it ever be different?
Must I return to the drudgery,
sacrificing what I have found of late?

Are there other options?

The Dreads

I hate this feeling,
this impending return to what
was my life,
grinding day after day, working until I
die.

You do what you have to,
taking the job so you can have insurance for the family,
so you can make the mortgage payment,
the car payment,
pay the power bill,
the phone bill,
the water bill,
the credit cards you use when the crap job doesn't pay
enough for the
other bills
so you borrow to pay, then pay what you
borrowed…
blah blah blah.
Rat race,
treadmill,
the hamster wheel of modern life.

Were we happier without it?
I mean, sure, life
expectancy was less, but why live to be 100 if you're
hating the life you have?
The daily struggle was
finding/killing food,

not going to the meaningless
job through lemming traffic.

I don't know,
maybe you are one of the lucky few
that was able to find fulfillment in your work.
A doctor or nurse able to help people every day,
or a baker feeding the hungry.
A retail worker assisting
customers with their needs and paid a decent wage,
able to support a family on what you bring home in
pay.
I hope you are.
I hope you love your job, most
of us don't.

Many of us lost that good job we loved
when the big banks and Wall Street screwed us in the
mortgage
meltdown in 2008.
Some of us face financial ruin
due to accident or injury,
sometimes by
circumstances not of our making.

Rambling,
disjointed,
and incoherent.
Struggling to find the motivation to return to work
without the hope of fulfillment or any type of progress.
But that treadmill keeps moving,

the hamster wheel spins,
just wish there was some way to get off,
to free myself from…this…

Shaving

The water ran
      Hot
and steaming over my hands
      Burning
my skin and clouding my image
      Blurring
my vision as I tried to find
      Myself.

I saw my face in the
      Mirror
but I could not find my
      Soul,
my visage showing the growth of
      Trouble
a legacy of needs unmet, ambition
      Unfulfilled.

The cold blade forged of
      Pain,
      Cut
through the wilderness of
      Confusion,
      Revealing
the nature of me, the loneliness of
      I.

A Thing of the City

I have become too much a thing of the city,
The fetid air rises from the heated stripes and lashes across
the good Earth.
Monuments to vain emptiness obscure heavenly light,
Overshadowing the denizens of this wretched realm.
Shadows deepen in the cloistered caves of the city,
Night moves in from the east.
Man's fear falsely illumines the darkened, forgotten souls
of meaner streets.

Where have the wondrous nights of my youth so soon fled?
Do the fiddlers of the moon no longer chirp their resonant
lay?
Why have peace and security left me on the wings of
unrealized tomorrow?

Running Time

44

Floating like driftwood in the river of time,
rolling toward waterfalls, spraying and scattering the light
into
brilliant
rainbows of gold, silver, and emerald.
Colors mingle with emotions, joining thoughts while the
world takes on brighter hues.
Flowers smell of blue and yellow, emotion scenting the air.
Winds lofting leaves of consciousness, expanding the mind,
Universal
Complete
Total awareness

Darkness

45

Velvet shrouds gently cradle a sapphire dream,
star-streaked horizons
flaming over countless citizens of a forgotten shore.
Night rides on a fiery chariot in the west,
Carried away by rosy sails of dawn.
Solace fills the void,
serenity giving no quarter to emptiness.
In the embrace of gentle night,
Resting in a diamond-studded shroud,
peace rolling over me in silken waves.

Air Pollution

Born into a world with no prejudice,
No concept of hate, no taint of malice,
All lost, polluted by the fetid air of society.
The young flower slowly opens to a new day,
reaching ever higher for nourishment from a pale sun.
Weak light cannot penetrate an ever-thickening haze,
cannot bless the earth with warmth.
Struggling to reach a dim future, the flower takes what
strength it can
from the fading light.
Could only the fabled winds of Aeolus now blow,
would a strong east wind come and reveal a
heaven so long hidden.

Digitized

Everything is digital now,
I can't hear the tick, tick, tick
Of a clock counting the hours
Until we see you again, time passes
Unnoticed through the night
Waiting for the dawn and the sound of
Your arrival to share the ritual of a
Normal day filled with simple joys.
Distracting myself with white noise
Background to fill the empty spaces
Soon occupied with what I have dreamed.

A Sign

Maybe it was a sign, a signal,
Some seemingly unrelated thing to let me know,
To change my course and set out into the unknown
Future I so long had dreamed.
I did not want to go back,
Did not want to fall into what was my life,
A dreary existence I hoped behind me.
The truck wouldn't start.
The battery was dead and would not charge.
A sign not to return to a place I didn't belong?
I tried to go back, I tried to jump it,
But I could not make it work.
So now I must choose, must decide,
Do I sail into an uncertain sea,
A fog-shrouded unknown spreading vast before me?
Do I now chart my new course?
Do I dare?
What choice do I have?

All on Christmas Day

It's Christmas Day,
I hear the children crying,
As the cold winds blow,
I see a nation dying.
A silent snow falls
Covering the graves of the slain,
Violence and fear still grips our world,
And man has cause to lament again.
I saw the children crying,
I heard a nation dying, all on Christmas Day.

Candle

50

"Be yourself" rings across the land, encouraging,
Be secure in your own identity.
Yet when honesty prevails, and the true self shines through,
Beautiful in its truth,
Truth is revealed or ignored.
The candle is despised by the darkness around it.

Cruel Time

Time exercises his cruel mastery over all,
Forcing submission from both great and small.
But love stands firm,
Scoffing at the cruel hours,
Love pushes through the gale,
Bright as the sun, gentle as the flower.

Race on cruel time,
Steal away today,
Yet shall I wait upon love,
Never to accept a lonely fate.

Fight It

I have to fight this.
I can't let it slip through my fingers again.
I must find a candle to push back the darkness creeping into
my mind.
I have to push through the thickening haze holding me
back.
I must keep doing me, the new me, the better me, the
expressive,
feeling, caring
Me.
I can't go back to stony hardness,
unable to grasp the small joys of being.
I won't stop fighting.
I can't freeze and wait,
seeking validation for what I now have become.
I will continue through the malaise,
crushing the breath from my dreams.
I will follow the feeble light I lit,
use my last breath to fan the flame of hope.
I must.
There is no other way.

Flying Falling Soft Landing

The opening lets the wind whip past my watering eyes,
Gazing into the azure abyss beckoning me to jump into the
unknown.
Hesitant, I raise one foot and then push off with the other.
Weightless, I fly.
Twisting through the air, I embrace the freedom,
Exulting in the rush of oxygen, speeding my synapses to
new connections,
I roll and see the clouds above me, fluffy pillows promising
rest,
Spinning I see the earth far below, greens and browns in
infinite variety,
I use my arms as wings, steering in the emptiness,
The ground rushes up,
Still I glory in the thrill of flying without limit,
Caution calling me to pull the cord, to secure the landing
anticipated,
I hesitate. I don't pull it. I push fear aside.
Dare I embrace the unknown?
Do I pull, or do I leave it all behind?
Enjoy the ride as long as I can until it suddenly ends,
Pull the co…

Graduation

54

'Twas a fair morn' indeed,
When my eyes swept o'er the sea,
No storm or warning skies beheld.
She was the good ship Hope,
Held in port with weathered rope,
As I stood on her bow to set my course.
The wind filled the sails,
The sun echoed our hails,
And I set out on track with Fate.
But the gentle wind turned bitter,
The mast began to shake and splinter,
And Hope was dashed 'gainst the
Jagged rocks of Cape Reality.

Hanging the Thread

It's just one of those silly little friendship bracelets
(get something more)
Just a little piece of thread I wore to make her happy
(constant reminder of what I secretly swore)
Time to move on, take it off and pursue others
(remove a piece of my soul for what cannot be)
Hang it on the mirror with other little doo-dads
(put it away like so many others gone from my life)

I hear myself try to brush it off, and I know I am lying,
Even though it is over, still I sit,
Alone and crying.

How Easily I Could Fall

56

How easily could I fall for you,
How quickly I could lose myself in your eyes,
Spinning round and round, holding you close as we dance
under a
crystal sky.
I could dream of you as I lie on the empty bed,
Wish for your gentle hand in mine while music plays softly
across
our bodies.
I could hope to taste your kiss in the morning light,
Long to feel your silky soft skin on mine,
Pray to smell your fragrance lingering on my pillow.
Oh yes, how easily I could fall in love with you.

How Far?

Are you that far away?
I can call and hear your voice in a moment,
The miles between us brushed away with a caress of you
speaking
my name.
How much of a fool can I be?
What madness is it that grips me?
These thoughts have begun to torment me as once before,
Like a commercial for the military reserves;
"One weekend a month, two weeks a year."
Can I let myself hope again?
Do I dare?

Falling Like Water

I can't regulate it,
I have tried to control it and failed miserably,
When the words come tumbling down,
The flow runs like a river over the cliffs at Niagara.
Sometimes, it is quite beautiful,
But in that beauty is pain.
In that flowing, sweeping expanse of vocabulary are barbs and rocks
Which, if taken wrong, can bring pain unexpressable.
I apologize, but I cannot prevent.
I regret, but I cannot remove the hurt.
The flow comes from somewhere beyond,
From without myself it seems,
The emotion set down in word as a composer sets it to music.
I do not mean to injure,
I do not mean to put salt in wounds unknown to me,
I write.
I just write.

In the Lonely Night

In the lonely night, a whiff of your fragrance stabbed me from a
fragment of memory,
Bringing the loneliness out of its hidden recess,
A demon rising from a gloomy cave.

A tear falls silently onto my pillow,
As visions of you once again dance before me.
The fragrance you wear wafts over the night winds,
Filling me with pain in each breath.
Tonight, I sleep alone and miserable,
Apart from the one I hold so dear,
Knowing that you sleep beside another,
No love to warm the marriage bed.
I hurt, my soul is tortured by multiplied agonies as I toss without
you,
Praying that you will not forget whose heart cries alone.

JoyPin

Some would call it gray,
I prefer silver,
A silver crown on a brow of ivory, being enchanted in the air.
I shouldn't miss you this much,
But my thoughts turn to you all too often.
Your fragrance lingers in memory,
Your phantom touch quickens my beating heart,
Your voice from afar brightens the darkest night.
A family incomplete without you,
Time dragging by in your absence
Your laughter speeding the minutes away.
My thoughts inevitably turn to more intimate moments,
Shared caresses, left and right, soft kisses by three.
Silky skin touching under cover of darkness,
Gentle brushes across the tender canvas,
Easy movements over multiple sweets, icing on cupcakes tasty and
full.
We talk about our time together,
Times not yet known, only hoped for.
Until we are together with you once more,
Know that our thoughts follow you ever,
Memory and anticipation of what may one day be.

Love Haiku

Breath so whisper soft
Caressing my cheek at night
Safe haven and rest

* * *

Golden rose petals
Falling silently to rest
On a lover's brow

* * *

Drifting off to sleep
Your head rests on my shoulder
Love misting my eyes

* * *

Winter's kiss at dawn
Lover's breath fogging the air
Held close on my breast

* * *

A harsh wind blows south
From mountains of memory
Cold and disturbing

Love Math

Love multiplies, it doesn't divide.
It is an infinite fountain,
Welling up from an endless source,
Filling our days with joy,
Towering over our pains like a mountain.
Love washes us over the rocky rapids of life,
Carries us along in its sparkling flows,
Crystal streams of majesty and grace,
Soaring like the eagle beyond far distant snows.
Love shines brightly in the darkness surrounding the fallen,
Burning the pain of loss and loneliness away,
Casting an anchor of hope into the troubled seas,
Promising like the dawn of a new, untroubled day.

Morning

While Apollo readies his chariot for the dawning sky,
As Luna surrenders her throne for another day of rest,
I wake to a cool breeze sighing through the pines.
A new journey beckons with uncertain course and distant
cry,
Siren song of what may yet be.
Behind lies the detritus of what was a good life, a nice
home, family,
No blame attaches to them for what now must become real,
No fault is theirs.
I set out alone to claim this new place,
This new land so long sought after yet never attained,
Alone to spare loved ones the pain of failures still possible,
The loss of the bird in hand reaching for the two in a far-off
bush.
Not weighted down, no, but not wanting to pull others
Into the maelstrom I see before me.
Supportive, helpful, loving,
Undeserving of the distress I may cause on this perilous
trek.

No Prophet I

64

I am no prophet,
No oracle can come and show me tomorrow or next week,
My choices must be my own,
My life shaped by my own hands.
But know this, though the road ahead carry me from your side,
The memory of your eyes and your touch will ever be my guide.
Wherever life carries us, together or apart,
I am yours always.
Though heaven burns and earth melts away,
I will never forget you.
Only one thing do I ask,
Will you remember me?

Placed in Grandma's Casket

I remember her cooking on the old stove with hands strong
and sure;
Hands that picked the corn and peas and what-all that went
into the
world's best vegetable soup;
Hands that held mine while she talked of gardens and days
now past;
Hands that held me in her lap as she read to a small boy
who felt safe
in her embrace;
Hands that rested gently on a fevered brow
in the dark summer night while prayers reached heaven;
Hands that held so many up in faith and conviction
unshaken.

I watched age take its inevitable toll,
Twisting those hands so gentle,
I saw time and illness conspire to take her away.

But I close my eyes and see her as she was,
and is:
Standing on the steps,
calling to a young man going away,
"Grandma loves you! You be a good boy!"

I will, Grandma, I will.

Playing Through the Pain

Going through the motions,
Making the merry music for others,
Putting up a brave front while holding back the tears.
Hands running over the ivory keys,
Music welling from the hammered strings in a locked
coffin,
Wanting only to match the sounds to my sorrow.
Lifting voices in song,
Crying out within for my loss,
Hoping my cry is heard by someone higher than I.

The Return

Tonight, I return to my happy place
(that's sarcasm)
Like so many others, I now do what I must to provide for
my family,
Must work for the little pieces of paper which make
modern life possible.
But more than that, the 800-pound gorilla you have to have
around.
(*INSURANCE*)
The inevitable difficulties of health plague all,
The troubles of age carry us into the antiseptic realms
unwelcome,
Which here comes with a cost directly taken from our
pound of flesh.
Pontificating heads in the media speak endlessly,
Immune to the concerns of the common folk,
Vaccinated by their wealth from the adversity facing the
majority
populace.
And so, like most, I return.
I force my body to perform, my soul aching for freedom
from this burdensome place.

Shorelines

Alone, I sit on a rocky shore,
Salt spray misting in the air around me,
The taste of the sea on my lips brings memory to mind,
A bitter rehashing of past mistakes and failings,
Cruel daggers of thought stabbing as the waves crash
against the dark
rocks below.
The roar of a distant wind pushing the water onto the land,
Storms over the horizon portend difficulty days ahead.

Alone, I stand on a sandy beach,
Gulls crying overhead in a symphony unwritten,
Gentle breezes carry the scent of ocean majesty to my
senses,
Promise of a new day ahead.
Dawn's rosy light colors the eastern sky with brilliance,
Walking into a bright tomorrow unfettered by a heavy past,
Forgotten the what-ifs and could-have-beens of yesterday,
Embracing the possible bright what-ifs and maybes of
tomorrow,
Rhythmic waves washing, cleaning, clearing a path to
travel.

Stop the Music

I stopped the music to listen to the night,
Low, dark clouds scurried past on cooler winds,
Reminder and promise rustling the treetops.
A hidden sun setting low in the west highlights a break in
the overcast sky,
Dancing across the yard quietly testifying "I'll be back
tomorrow."
Stronger winds blow, and the clouds close in,
Night slowly approaches from the east.
A small smile sneaks across my face,
And I rest content.

The Spring Behind My House

There was a spring behind my house.
The water welled up constantly from the deep,
Drawing all manner of life from nearby.
The squirrels would come down from the towering oaks,
Scampering about, leaving tiny tracks in the mud.
The owl sat silently watching as the chipmunks and other
Small creatures danced and darted around the water's
Crystal edge.
Deer came to slake their thirst,
Finding refuge beneath the canopy of oak, beech, and bay,
Snorting as the turkeys went to roost overhead.
I would sit and watch, happy, and
Marvel at the beauty of the little spring.

The timber is sold.
The land is raped and scarred.
The trees taken to make paper, and cabinets,
And maybe a $14.99 coffee table.

There was once a little
Spring behind my house.

There I Stood

I stood by your side when you needed me,
Supported you in every detail,
And I let you walk away when you wanted,
No matter how much it hurt.
I stood by and watched with worry and pain,
Waiting until fate brought you into my life again.
I think it was your eyes.
And now, after so many restless nights and stolen kisses,
Dreams of us and shadowed fancies,
Now, we are us.
Now when I gaze into your eyes,
I see love in those sky-blue depths.
Definitely, your eyes.
Not now the burning flower of youth, but a purer thing,
Tempered by wisdom and forged in common pain.

Unrequited

The chairs are empty now,
The lights still flash,
The music still plays,
But I'm alone again.
I can see you across the room, close enough
To catch your perfume on each stirring of the smoky air,
Sitting with another who has better claim.
No demon in hell could torment me more,
No sadist devise a more painful torture,
Yet here I sit,
Held tight in an embrace I know only from my dreams,
Wrapped in chains of desire so strong,
Bound by a need I cannot deny.
Trapped by hope,
I watch you leave with him,
Sitting in the darkness with my phantoms,
My mind trying to free my heart from its gilded prison.

Wanting Waiting Yearning

I have felt your touch in my dreams,
Your hands caressing my back in the night,
Your sweet kiss brushing my lips in the cool of the
morning.
Too many nights have I lain awake wanting you by my
side,
Hours passed in endless longing.
I want to feel your soft, soft, skin on mine,
Feel your breath against my neck,
Stroke your golden locks with my hand,
Holding you close.
I will be your place of comfort,
Your refuge from all life's storms.
I will ease the pain you feel and be whatever you need,
If only you let me within the walls you have built.
For that night I wait,
When finally you will be mine and I yours,
Completely and gladly.

What I Am

What am I? How am I defined?
Am I more than what I make?
Is my value determined by the return on a capital
investment?
Am I only valuable if I produce some product for
consumption by an indifferent system?
Do I serve a purpose only in service to a predetermined
end, a goal not my own?
What am I?

I am a father,
> Two smart, talented, beautiful little girls depend on
> me to "Daddy."
>> (One of them not so little anymore)

I am a husband,
> A wonderful woman completes me, supports me,
> makes each day a journey worth taking.

I am a son, a brother, an uncle, a friend.
I am a piano player, making music to help heal the broken
and lift the downtrodden,
music to accompany people in their joys and sorrows.
I am a writer, putting words to paper conveying thoughts
and emotion for folk to ponder.

I am defined and valuated by my relationship with other
human beings defined by their own relationships.

Cogito Ergo Sum

We think,
We feel,
We love,
Therefore we are.

The Calculus of Hate

Hate divides, ad infinitum,
Reducing, diminishing all it touches,
Decimating hearts and lives until nothing remains.
Hate thrashes its way across landscapes, both foreign and
familiar,
Vaporizing relationships, ending everything in its path.

But eventually, Hate fails, having reached the indivisible.
With no more fuel for it's rages,
It fades away into emptiness and pain.

The Generation Between

I have begun to stop and just check on them each morning,
On my way to work, I'll swing by and make sure
everything is OK,
See what doctor's appointments are on the schedule.
They are both in their 80s now, thankfully in pretty good
health, all things considered.
But still, I worry, especially since my last uncle passed
away,
Leaving my father without siblings in this world.
My mother seems to be doing better after recent health
issues.
But still, I worry.

My oldest is beginning her journey,
Applications, interviews,
Starting on the career path we all have to travel,
She'll be fine, I know,
But still, I worry.
The youngest is doing well in school,
Good reports and seemingly on the way to being the
valedictorian,
Her mother and I are very proud, of course,
She practices her French horn, her archery, piano and choir,
We try to keep up, but still, I worry.

The wife runs after our daughter,
Taking her to practices, Taking care of the meds and
appointments for the entire family,

Running the household while I go to work each day, doing
my thing,
But still, I worry.

Sandwiched between aging parents and growing children,
Pulled and stretched, candles burned from both ends,
We're hanging in there
but still, I worry.

About the Author

J. R. Cleckler graduated from the University of Alabama with a bachelor's degree in history/English, with a minor in political science. A planned future in academia was set aside, and many years in retail ensued. The recent events with the pandemic provided the time and opportunity to pursue a dream of writing. He is the father of two wonderful girls and the husband of a beautiful and supportive wife.